Howard B. Wigglebottom

Learns About Courage

Howard Binkow

Reverend Ana

Jeremy Norton

Scholastic Canada Ltd.

Toronto New York London Auckland Sydney
Mexico City New Delhi Hong Kong Buenos Aires

Howard Binkow
Reverend Ana
Illustration by Jeremy Norton
Special thanks to Warren Muzak
Book design by Jane Darroch Riley

Thunderbolt Publishing
We Do Listen Foundation
www.wedolisten.org

Gratitude and appreciation are given to all those who reviewed the story prior to publication;
the book became much better by incorporating several of their suggestions:

Teachers, librarians, counselors and students at:

Bossier Parish Schools, Bossier City, Louisiana
Chalker Elementary, Kennesaw, Georgia
Charleston Elementary, Charleston, Arkansas
Cummings Elementary School, Misawa Air Force Base, Japan
Forest Avenue Elementary, Hudson, Massachusetts
Garden Elementary, Venice, Florida
Glen Alpine Elementary, Morganton, North Carolina
Golden West Elementary, Manteca, California
Hartsdale Avenue Public School, Mississauga, Ontario, Canada

Iveland Elementary School, St. Louis, Missouri
Kincaid Elementary, Marietta, Georgia
Lamarque Elementary School, North Port, Florida
Lee Elementary, Los Alamitos, California
Sherman Oaks Elementary, Sherman Oaks, California
Victoria Avenue Elementary, South Gate, California
Walt Disney Magnet School, Chicago, Illinois
West Navarre Primary, Navarre, Florida

ISBN 978-1-4431-1969-6

6 5 4 3 2 1   Printed in Singapore 46   13 14 15 16 17

This book belongs to

_____

Nobody knew why Howard B. Wigglebottom had
been so afraid the past few weeks. He just wasn't
himself. He was scared of the dark and what could be

. . . he was scared of toilets, loud noises and high places. He crossed the street whenever he saw strange people and dogs.

He stopped playing outside altogether because of the possibility of seeing spiders and snakes.

But most of all he feared the first day of school.

7

When he decided not to leave his room ever again, his friends and family became very worried.

One morning when he was looking outside the window, he saw a baby bird looking in.

"Are you here to watch my important moment?" asked the bird.
"It's my first day of learning how to fly."

"Oh! How are you going to do that?" asked Howard. "I thought all birds were born knowing how to fly."

"No, no. We learn only after we jump out of the nest," answered the bird.

"You don't even know if you can fly and you jump anyway? Aren't you afraid?" asked Howard.

"Yes, we get butterflies in our tummies from fear that our wings might not work – but we do it anyway," said the bird. "Watch me. Here I go."

"Wait!" Howard said. "Should I place something under the tree?" But before he could finish his question, the little bird jumped out of its nest.

"I did it! I did it! Look how high I can go!" said the bird. Howard was amazed. The bird was such a fast learner – and so BRAVE, too . . .

"I wish I could be more like you," said Howard. "Lately I am so afraid of everything – I'm not sure what's wrong with me."

"My mother says everybody is afraid of something," said the bird. "The reason we have fears is to learn about courage. If we are not afraid of anything, we can't have courage."

"So all superheroes are brave because they have fear but do what they have to do anyway?" asked Howard.

"Yes," said the bird. "If you're not afraid, you can't be BRAVE."

Howard liked the idea. Birds and superheroes were afraid, but that didn't stop them from doing what they wanted to do.
He could try that, too!

That night he smiled at the dark and the make-believe monsters and told himself, "It's OK to be afraid." He slept well all night! When he woke up, he decided to do the things he liked to do even if he was afraid. He wanted to get ready for his biggest fear: the first day at his new school.

He listened to loud noises, and it was OK. "I'm brave. I was afraid, but I did it anyway," Howard told himself.

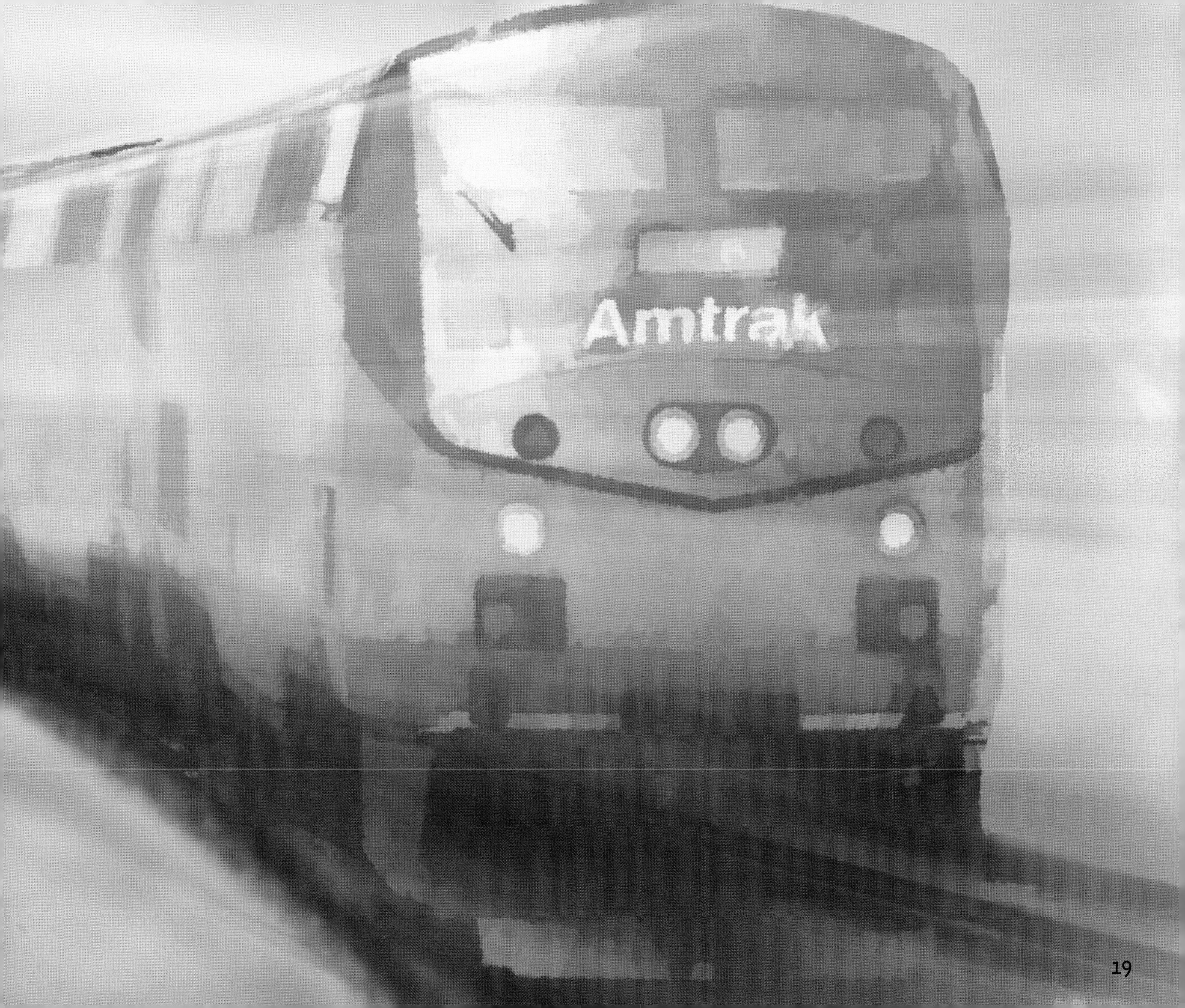
Amtrak

It's OK to be afraid

He asked his father to take him on a small plane ride, and he really liked it.

He went to a tall building with his mom and took the elevator all the way to the top and back down – it wasn't that bad at all.

At the zoo, he was very brave. Yes, the spiders and snakes were very frightening, but some of them could be pretty and cool, too. Howard told himself, "It's OK to be afraid."

Next, he asked his neighbour to teach him how to be friendly with a dog. Playing with his friends' dogs was fun! He was scared at first, but because he was brave, he did it anyway!

SECRETARY

28

Howard had so much fun taking care of each fear that, when the first day at his new school arrived, he had almost forgotten about it.

He met his new teacher, shook hands with the people at the office and cafeteria, and smiled at all the new boys and girls in his class.

Howard felt great!
All the while he told
himself, "I am brave.
I was afraid, but I did
it anyway!"